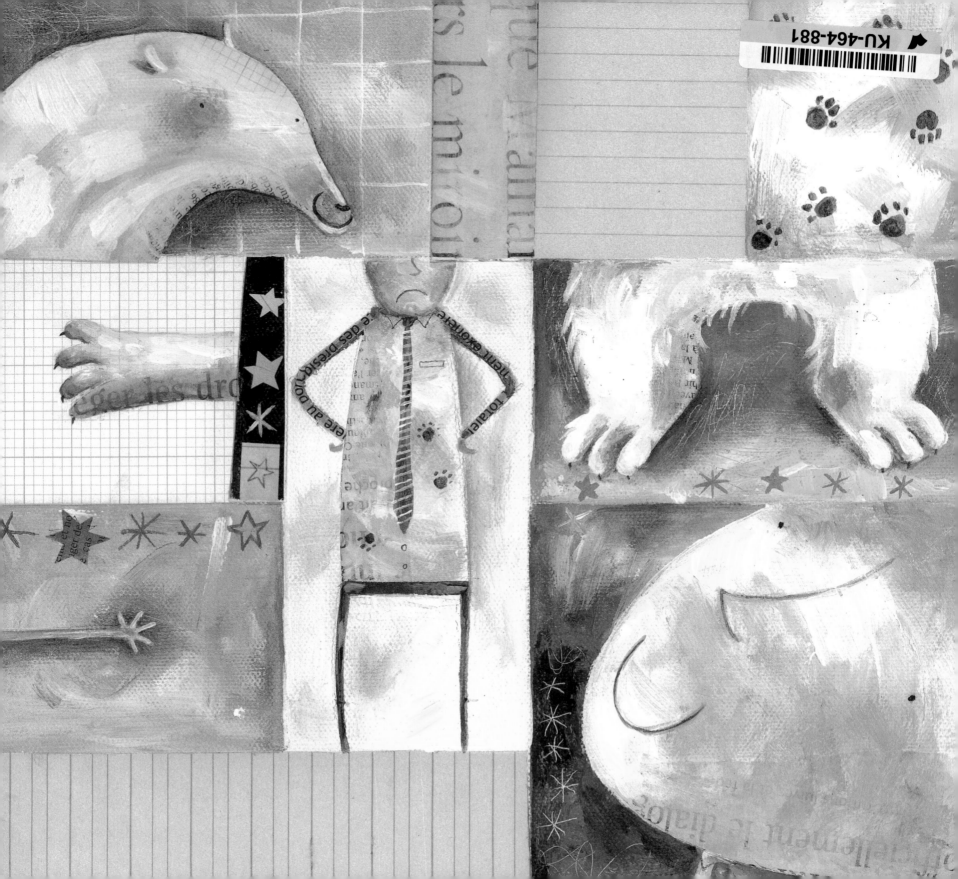

For my dad
(who remembered the *Titanic* sinking) — PD

With love and thanks to
Mum, Dad, Ed and Floss — NC

DAD'S BUG BEAR
A RED FOX BOOK 978 0 099 47292 6 (from January 2007)
0 099 47292 9

First published in Great Britain in 2006 by Red Fox,
an imprint of Random House Children's Books
Text copyright © Peter Dixon, 2006
Illustrations copyright © Natalie Chivers, 2006
The right of Peter Dixon and Natalie Chivers
to be identified as the author and illustrator of
this work has been asserted in accordance with
the Copyright, Designs and Patents Act 1988.
Random House Children's Books,
61–63 Uxbridge Road, London W5 5SA
A division of The Random House Group Ltd
All rights reserved. 1 3 5 7 9 10 8 6 4 2
The Random House Group Limited Reg. No. 954009
www.kidsatrandomhouse.co.uk
A CIP catalogue record for this book is available from the British Library
Printed in China

Peter Dixon

Dad's Bug Bear

Natalie Chivers

RED FOX

Dad did not like pets.

He said cats **miaowed** too much,

dogs **ate** too much

and mice made him **itch**.

I had a goldfish.
His name was Frank.

Dad said Frank was **smelly.**

One morning I found Frank floating
on top of his bowl.

He was dead.

'Oh dear,' said Mum.

'Never mind,
son,' said Dad.
   'Tell you what,'
said Mum.
   'You can have
a cheer-up treat.
What would you
like to do?'

   'Go to the zoo!'
I said.

Dad looked fed up.
'But I don't like zoos,'
he moaned.

'I **don't like** camels,

I **don't like** elephants.

Giraffes' necks are too **long.**

Seals are too **slithery.**

Penguins are too **wobbly**

and rhinos are too **knobbly!'**

'Too bad.
It's not your treat,'
said Mum.

So off we went.

But when we arrived . . . Oh, dear!

Disaster!

'I am sorry, sir,' said the keeper.
'But two African elephants
pushed down the walls
and all the animals
have escaped.'

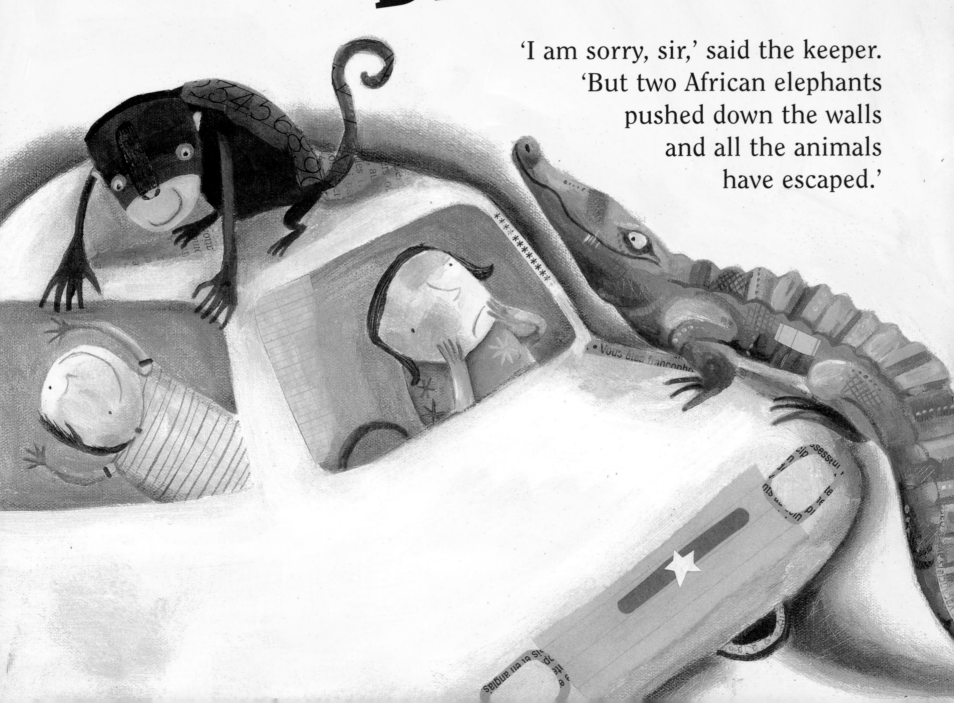

'**Rotten African elephants!**'
said Dad. 'I hope no runaway animals
go anywhere near *our* house.
We'd better hurry home.'

The roads
were very busy.
I kept thinking about
Frank and still felt very sad.
'Can I have a new pet?'
I asked hopefully.

'I'm sorry, son,' said Dad.
'You know I don't like animals.
But you've still got the water
snail in Frank's bowl,'
he added, trying to
cheer me up.

FISH
'n'
CHIPS

At last we got home,
but as I walked towards
the front door, I saw
something
very nasty
on the step.

'**What is it?**'
asked Mum.

'**Oh no!**'
cried Dad.
'It's polar bear poo –
that's what that is.

**I hate rotten
polar bears!**'

Dad got a spade and threw the poo over the fence.

I sat with my water snail.
I decided to call her Rosemary.

But I still felt sad about Frank.

At bath time I took Rosemary with me.
The water was warm and bubbly and Rosemary
was crawling around looking for Frank.
I was beginning to feel happier
when suddenly I heard

a creak, a snap, a roar, and then . . .

Mum rushed in.
'Oh dear!'
she cried.
'I'll run and get
your father!'

Help! Help!
Fire brigade!
Police!

'What's the matter now?' sighed Dad. 'As soon as I start watching the telly someone always wants me to do something!'

He hurried upstairs.

'**Eeek!**
It's a great big
polar bear leg
that's what that is!' said Dad.

And he tapped it
with the toilet brush.

'**Grrrr!**'
went the bear.

The police came,
then the fire brigade
and then the keepers
from the zoo.

By this time the bear was up on our roof. And he wouldn't budge.

'He's smashing my new roof tiles!' cried Dad.

'Hey, get down!'

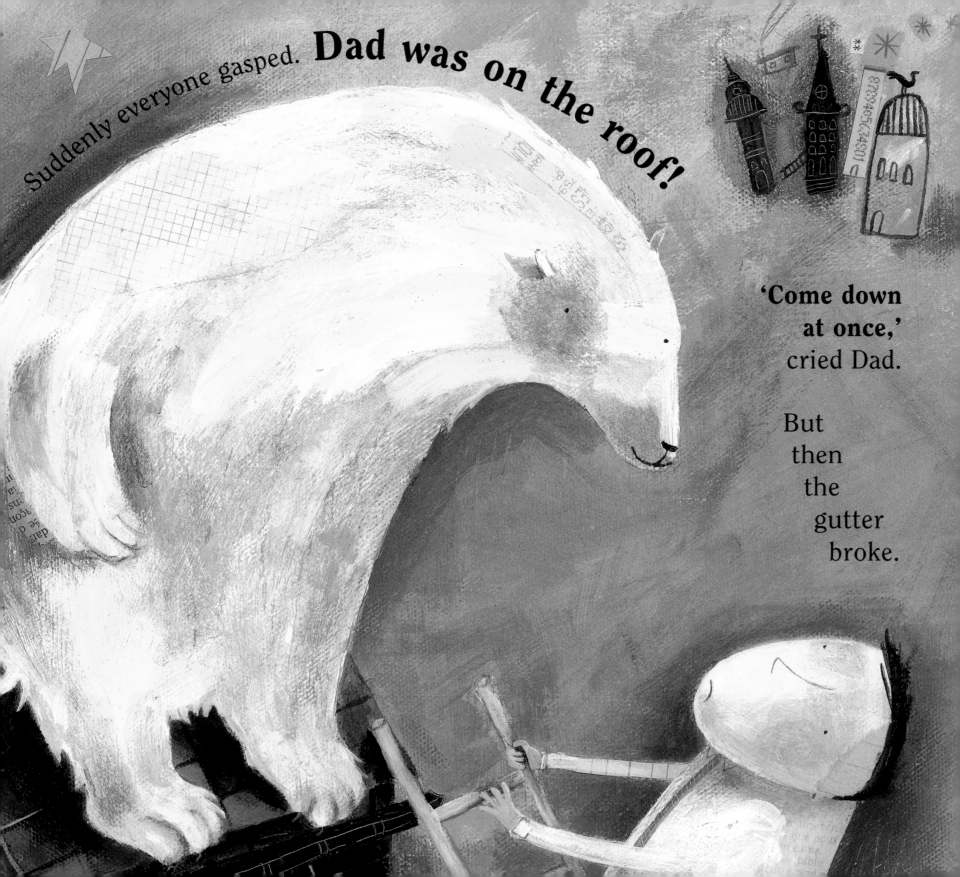

Suddenly everyone gasped. **Dad was on the roof!**

'Come down
at once,'
cried Dad.

But
then
the
gutter
broke.

Down went the gutter!

Down went the bear!

Down went the ladder!

Then down came

Dad...

Right into the big furry arms of the bear!

**'Well done!'
cried everyone.**

'Good blooming
catch!' gasped Dad.

'Come along,
Bertie,' said
the keeper.
'It's time to go
back to the zoo.'

Slowly and gently the
great bear was driven away.

We all felt sad.
'I suppose he wasn't a
bad old chap,' said Dad.

Then he smiled.
'Tell you what we'll do!
We'll go back to the
zoo tomorrow and
check he's OK.'

'Hooray!' I cried.
'Dad likes animals after all.'
'I only said I liked polar bears,' said Dad.

'I don't like   **itchy** mice,   African elephants   or those
whiskery walruses,   **sloppy** sea lions,   **pesky** penguins,

they can give you a nasty nip!'

We all smiled.

Mum looked at me.

'I think we could
all do with a
nice cool drink
from the fridge,'
she said.

'Hooray!' I cried.
'Dad likes animals after all.'
'I only said I liked polar bears,' said Dad.

'I don't like   *itchy* mice,   African elephants   or those
whiskery walruses,   sloppy sea lions,   pesky penguins,

they can give you a nasty nip!'

We all smiled.

Mum looked at me.

'I think we could
all do with a
nice cool drink
from the fridge,'
she said.

'Hooray!' I cried.

'Dad likes animals after all.'
'I only said I liked polar bears,' said Dad.

'I don't like **itchy mice,** African elephants or those
whiskery walruses, **sloppy sea lions,** **pesky penguins,**

they can give you a nasty nip!'

We all smiled.

Mum looked at me.

'I think we could
all do with a
nice cool drink
from the fridge,'
she said.

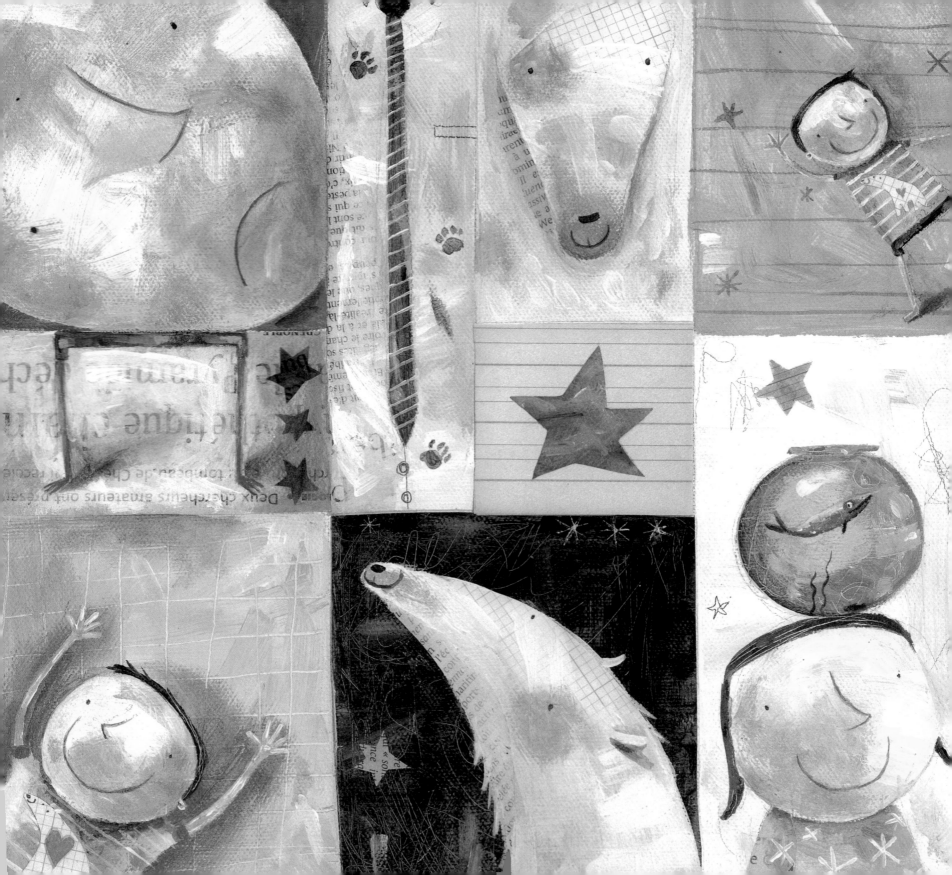

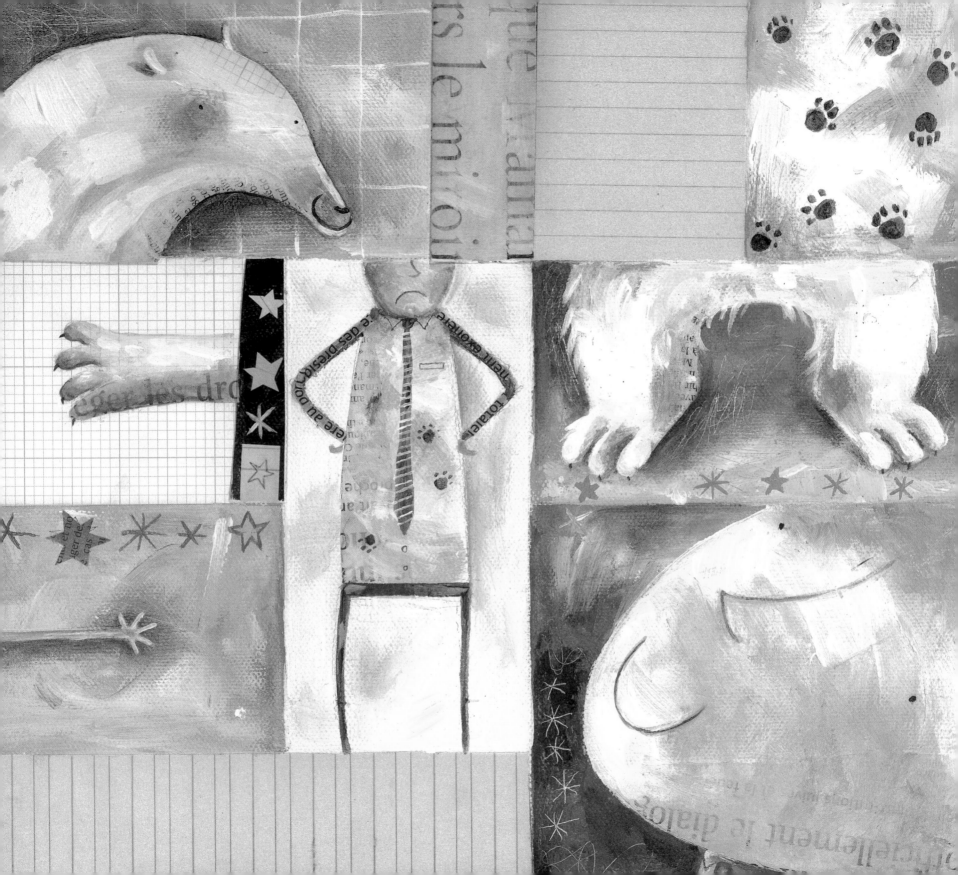

Other books you might enjoy:

Slow Loris
BY ALEXIS DEACON

My Dad
BY ANTHONY BROWNE

Amazing Animal Hide and Seek
BY JOHN ROWE

Polly Jean Pyjama Queen
BY STEVE WEBB

Two Frogs
BY CHRIS WORMELL

Billy's Bucket
BY KES GRAY AND GARRY PARSONS